Tomie dePaola
Country Angel Christmas

Scholastic Inc.
New York Toronto London Auckland Sydney

For Martha and Ralph

ISBN 0-590-97505-6

Copyright © 1995 by Tomie dePaola.
All rights reserved. Published by Scholastic Inc., 555 Broadway, New York, NY 10012,
by arrangement with G.P. Putnam's Sons, a division of The Putnam & Grosset Group.

12 11 10 9 8 7 6 5 4 3 2 1   6 7 8 9/9 0 1/0

Printed in the U.S.A.   08

First Scholastic printing, September 1996

"Look," shouted Ari.
"It's St. Nicholas!" Pip exclaimed.
"But it's not Christmas Eve," Kira said.

"Why are you here so early?" Harim, the Head Angel, asked. "I have exciting news! You have been chosen to make the Christmas celebration for all of Heaven this year!"

The Country Angels didn't say a word. They didn't smile. Not even Ari, Pip and Kira, the youngest angels who were always chattering and asking questions.

"What's the matter?" St. Nicholas asked.

"Oh, St. Nicholas," Harim said. "We aren't important enough for such a big occasion. Last year the Archangels made Heaven sparkle with gold and silver."

"And the year before, the Heavenly Choir made Christmas with harps and trumpets, and hundreds of voices singing in a magnificent chorus. What could we do that would be good enough?" asked Petra, the Music Angel.

"Ah," St. Nicholas said. "Don't think about what others have done. Just be yourselves and you will make a fine Christmas. You'll see."

The next day the Country Angels met in the barn.
"What St. Nicholas said is true," Harim said. "We
must all do what we do best."

"We can offer wonderful things to eat from our
kitchens," said Adasa, the Kitchen Angel.
"Let's have a procession with our animals," said Nebo
and Ziph, the Barn Angels. Everyone began having ideas
at once for wreaths of holly, banners of silk in all the
heavenly colors, and songs for everyone to sing.

"But not in parts," said Petra, the Music Angel.
"It will be glorious," they all called out.
"What can WE do?" shouted Ari, Pip and Kira.
"The best thing you can do is stay out of the way,"
the angels told them.

The next day Ari, Pip and Kira went to the kitchen where angels were peeling and sifting, pouring and stirring.
"Can we help?"
"Shoo!" said Adasa. "You'll just make a mess."

They went to the angels who were cutting pine branches, measuring ribbons, and collecting holly for the wreaths.

"What can we do?" they asked.

"You're too young to do anything," Aram said.

"May we wind the thread on the spools?" they asked Midda.
"You'll only tangle it all up," Midda told them.

And when they tried to make music with the Music Angels,
they were too fast or too slow.

Finally, Ari, Pip and Kira went to the barn where they often played with the animals.

But even Nebo and Ziph had no time for them when
they asked if they could help groom the animals.
"We have enough help," Ziph said.

On the day that St. Nicholas came to see how
the Country Angels were getting on, he found Ari, Pip
and Kira sitting outside the barn doing nothing.

"What's the matter?" St. Nicholas asked. "Aren't you
helping to get ready for Christmas?"

"Oh, St. Nicholas," they told him. "No one wants us to help with anything. They think we're too young."

"Hmmm," said St. Nicholas. "I think I have an idea. He gathered them close and whispered so that no one could hear.

On the morning of Christmas Eve before flying off
to Earth, St. Nicholas came with his sleigh. The Country
Angels filled it with fresh straw and pine boughs to keep
him warm on his journey. They put bright red quilts over
each reindeer and wound holly around their harnesses.

"I will be back this evening after I've visited all
the children and we'll have our Christmas together."
Ari, Pip and Kira smiled. They couldn't wait for
their surprise.

All that day the Country Angels worked.

No one noticed that Ari, Pip and Kira were nowhere to be seen.

It was dark when St. Nicholas returned. The Archangels
and the Heavenly Choir and all of Heaven had gathered.
Everyone wanted to see what the Country Angels
had planned.

Everything was in place. The procession was ready to begin.
But the Country Angels were worried. It was getting darker
and darker and no one could see anything. "What shall we do?"
they whispered. They had forgotten that Christmas Eve is one
of the darkest nights of the year.

Then they heard a murmuring among the Archangels. "Look," said the Heavenly Choir. A glow had appeared across the sky and when the Country Angels turned around, they saw Ari, Pip and Kira pulling a large star across the Heavens.

"The Star of Bethlehem!" they cried.
The hillside shone with light.

"Oh, thank you, Ari, Pip and Kira," all the angels said. "You must lead the procession." And the three smallest angels started up the hill with the bright star above them lighting up all of Heaven.

Silent night, holy night. All is calm. All is bright.